Dear Parent:
Your child's love of reading starts here!

Every child learns to read in a different way and at his or her own speed. Some go back and forth between reading levels and read favorite books again and again. Others read through each level in order. You can help your young reader improve and become more confident by encouraging his or her own interests and abilities. From books your child reads with you to the first books he or she reads alone, there are I Can Read Books for every stage of reading:

SHARED READING
Basic language, word repetition, and whimsical illustrations, ideal for sharing with your emergent reader

BEGINNING READING
Short sentences, familiar words, and simple concepts for children eager to read on their own

READING WITH HELP
Engaging stories, longer sentences, and language play for developing readers

READING ALONE
Complex plots, challenging vocabulary, and high-interest topics for the independent reader

I Can Read Books have introduced children to the joy of reading since 1957. Featuring award-winning authors and illustrators and a fabulous cast of beloved characters, I Can Read Books set the standard for beginning readers.

A lifetime of discovery begins with the magical words **"I Can Read!"**

Visit www.icanread.com for information
on enriching your child's reading experience.

Visit www.zonderkidz.com/icanread for more faith-based
I Can Read! titles from Zonderkidz.

ZONDERKIDZ

I Can Read Fiona Saves the Day
Copyright © 2021 by Zondervan
Illustration: © 2021 by Zondervan

An **I Can Read Book**

Requests for information should be addressed to:
Zonderkidz, 3900 Sparks Drive SE, Grand Rapids, Michigan 49546

Hardcover ISBN 978-0-310-77098-5
Softcover ISBN 978-0-310-77097-8
Ebook ISBN 978-0-310-77099-2

Library of Congress Cataloging-in-Publication Data
Names: Cowdrey, Richard, illustrator.
Title: Fiona saves the day / illustrations by Richard Cowdrey.
Description: Grand Rapids : Zonderkids, [2021] | Series: I can read. Level
   1 | Audience: Ages 4-8 | Summary: Fiona the Hippo and her friends at the
   zoo come together to help Mango, a little blue penguin who is stuck on a
   ledge.
Identifiers: LCCN 2020026515 (print) | LCCN 2020026516 (ebook) | ISBN
   9780310770985 (hardcover) | ISBN 9780310770978 (paperback) | ISBN
   9780310770992 (epub)
Subjects: CYAC: Animal rescue--Fiction. | Hippopotamus--Fiction. | Zoo
   animals--Fiction.
Classification: LCC PZ7.1.C685 Fio 2021 (print) | LCC PZ7.1.C685 (ebook)
   | DDC [E]--dc23
LC record available at https://lccn.loc.gov/2020026515
LC ebook record available at https://lccn.loc.gov/2020026516

Contributors: Jesse Doogan and Mary Hassinger
Art direction and design: Cindy Davis

I Can Read® and I Can Read Book® are trademarks of HarperCollins Publishers.

Printed in China

ZONDERkidz

Fiona Saves
the Day

New York Times Bestselling Illustrator
Richard Cowdrey
with Donald Wu

 ZONDERkidz

It was a sunny day at the zoo.
Fiona the Hippo was visiting
her friends.

4

She heard birds singing.
She watched monkeys playing catch
and cheetahs running.

Fiona stopped to see the tall giraffes.
They were looking for leaves to eat
high up in the trees.

Then Fiona went to visit the bears.
They picked up food with
their big paws.

Next, Fiona said hello to
the orangutans.

Some orangutans covered their heads
with blankets.
It was so hot in the sun.

Then Fiona went to
the penguin house.

She loved to watch the
penguins dive
and swim and waddle.

11

But today, the penguins
looked worried!
"What's wrong?" asked Fiona.

"It's Mango," said a king penguin.
"She's stuck on a ledge!"

Fiona looked up.

She saw the little blue penguin
named Mango.

"Oh no!" said Fiona.
"We have to help her!"

Mango was very high up.

"I will try to help you," said Fiona.

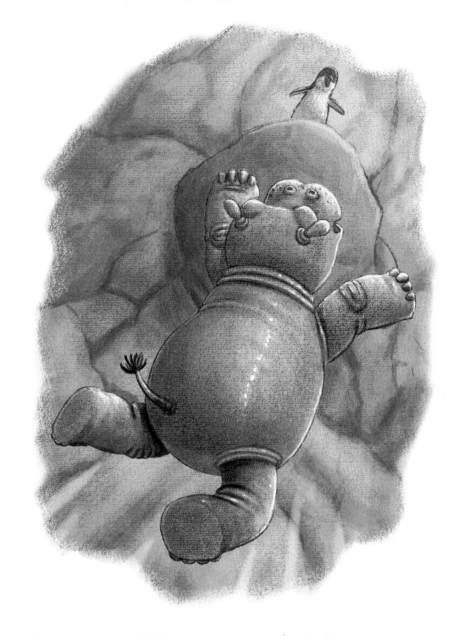

Fiona could not reach Mango
by jumping.
She could not climb up to get her.

Just then, Kris the cheetah came
to see what all the fuss was about.

"Kris," said Fiona.

"Mango is stuck!

We have to help her!"

"Yes! We need a plan!" said Kris.

"We will help you, Mango,"
called Fiona.

"Don't move."

Fiona and Kris walked.

They thought about a plan.

They saw animals in their homes.

The animals were using their
special talents.

They saw the monkeys and bear.

They saw the giraffe and orangutan.

Then Fiona had a good idea.

"I've got this," said Fiona,

as she wiggled her ears and snorted.

Fiona told Kris the cheetah her idea.

"Great idea, Fiona!" Kris said.

"I'll be back in a flash!"

Kris ran off.

Soon, he came back
with animal helpers.
He brought the bear, some monkeys,
the orangutan, and the giraffe.

"Okay," said Fiona.

"Here's the plan."

Fiona told the animals they
each had a job.

"We will work together.
We will use our talents
to help Mango. We've got this!"
Fiona said.

Fiona asked the orangutan
to share his blanket.
He gave his blanket to a monkey.
"We can use this as a hammock.
It will keep Mango safe," said Fiona.

Next, the bear picked up the monkeys.

He set them on Giraffe's back.

"That tickles!" said the giraffe.

The monkeys went up the giraffe's
neck to her head.

The two monkeys held the
blanket out.

"Jump into the blanket, Mango!"
called Fiona.

"We'll catch you," said the monkeys.

Mango jumped. She went
right into the blanket.
The giraffe lowered the monkeys
and Mango to the ground.

"Thanks for your help, everyone,"
said Mango.

"We did it together!" said Fiona.

Everyone cheered, "Hooray, Fiona!
Hooray for us! We've got this."